For Archie Ryder.

S.M.

For Penfold & Ringo.

T.M.

ORCHARD BOOKS
338 Euston Road, London NW1 3BH
Orchard Books Australia
Hachette Children's Books
Level 17/207 Kent St, Sydney, NSW 2000
ISBN 1 84362 570 9 (hardback)
ISBN 1 84362 803 1 (paperback)
First published in Great Britain in 2006
First paperback publication in 2007
Text © Sue Mongredien 2006
Illustrations © Teresa Murfin 2006
The rights of Sue Mongredien to be identified as the author
and of Teresa Murfin to be identified as the illustrator of this work
have been asserted by them in accordance with the
Copyright, Designs and Patents Act, 1988.
A CIP catalogue record for this book is available
from the British Library.
1 3 5 7 9 10 8 6 4 2 (hardback)
1 3 5 7 9 10 8 6 4 2 (paperback)
Printed and bound in Great Britain by
Mackays of Chatham plc, Chatham Kent
www.wattspublishing.co.uk

FRIGHTFUL FAMILIES

ASTRONERDS

Sue Mongredien • Teresa Murfin

ORCHARD BOOKS

Buzz Burton lived with his mum and dad
in a normal house, in a normal street, in
a normal town. Buzz was just like every other
boy – a bit scruffy, a bit cheeky and always
hungry. His mum and dad weren't like other
parents though. They were astronauts!

Everyone at school thought Buzz's parents were utterly cool. After all, nobody else had had a moon rock for their Christmas present.

And nobody else's holiday snaps were a patch on Mrs Burton's.

US ON THE MOON SUMMER '04

While other parents went to work by car, bike or bus, Buzz's parents travelled by space shuttle.

Even Buzz had to admit that was pretty cool. But there were plenty of other things about his parents that were *not* so cool. They loved their work so much that they were kind of *geeky* about it. Buzz sometimes called them 'the astronerds'.

He wished his dad would answer the phone properly.

Buzz just *cringed* if it was one of his friends phoning up.

And the way his parents insisted on using walkie-talkies around the house drove him nuts.

"Affirmative, Space Commander Sally. Two sugars, please. Over and out."

Still, deep down, Buzz was proud of his mum and dad. It was only when work for the *Venturer 5* mission got underway that their strangeness went into hyper-drive.

Venturer 5 was a brand new spacecraft, designed to orbit Venus and take photographs. Buzz's parents were going to be the first to fly it. And didn't Buzz know about it.

Ever since the trip had been announced, his mum and dad had talked of nothing else. They'd started a tough training programme.

They went power walking before breakfast.

And they mapped out their mission all morning. "So we turn right at the Moon..."

They studied their star charts all afternoon. "Such a cool constellation..."

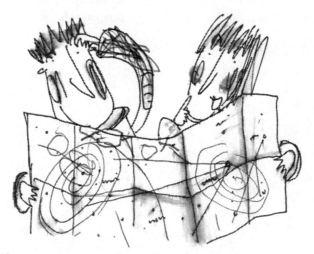

They even tested each other at tea-time.

Buzz knew they were just working hard at their jobs but he couldn't help wishing they didn't have to be so *weird* about it. Surely his mum didn't have to wear that awful home-made spacesuit around the house?

And the whole street was talking about
the towering treehouse his dad had built in
the garden. Why couldn't he and Mum just
keep the telescope in the house?

Still, Buzz had to admit that everyone was really impressed that Mr and Mrs Burton were going to Venus. And suddenly, *everyone* in the school wanted to come to Buzz's birthday party!

Buzz, on the other hand, did *not* want to go to his party. He was the only kid in school who was dreading the whole thing.

His mum was making an alien style cake with lurid green icing.

She was planning rocket-shaped rolls, Neptune nuggets, cosmonaut cookies and inter-galactic ice cream – whatever *that* was.

That, on its own, wasn't so bad. But then there was the two-hour moon video Dad wanted to show to Buzz's friends.

Mum had volunteered to demonstrate moonwalking to everybody.

And Dad had invented a 'comets and asteroids' game with hand-made costumes.

"Um...I think we might just play football, actually," Buzz said weakly a few times.

Buzz knew that once all his mates had spent an afternoon with the astronerds, he was sure to become the laughing stock of the school!

In no time at all, it was Buzz's birthday.

Buzz opened his eyes and blinked. There was his mum, with a breakfast tray. There was his dad, with a pile of presents. Excellent!

"Breakfast in bed," his mum smiled, passing it over. "And not just any old breakfast – an astronaut breakfast!"

Buzz stared at the contents of the tray. They didn't look very appetising.

"This foil packet is orange juice," his mum told him. "And I've mixed up some powdered scrambled egg for you. Oh, and this packet is dried cereal. Happy birthday, love!"

"Mmm, thanks, Mum," Buzz said, trying to look happy. His stomach rumbled in disappointment. He really hoped the party food would be better than this!

"And here are some presents," his dad said, putting them onto the bed.

Buzz grinned. He'd been dropping hints for weeks about the computer game he wanted.

After a few mouthfuls of flaky lukewarm egg, Buzz pretended to be full and opened the first present. It was a...

...telescope. "Great. Thanks," Buzz said, trying not to sigh.

The second present was *definitely* computer-game shaped. Buzz managed to open it with his fingers still crossed. It was a book about the solar system.

The third present was quite squashy. Buzz grinned. It had to be the football shirt he'd asked for! Or maybe a pair of jeans? He pulled off the paper. It was a...

...Oh, no. *No!* It was a home-made spacesuit, just like his mum's!

Buzz slurped his space juice because he didn't know what to say. "Wow," he managed to get out eventually. "You must have spent ages making this."

"I knew you'd like it," his mum said fondly. "Maybe we could both wear our spacesuits for the party this afternoon?"

"Yeah, maybe," Buzz said. And maybe *not*, he thought to himself. In fact, there was absolutely no *way* he was going to wear a handmade spacesuit to his own party. No way on Earth – or on any other planet!

Once Buzz's guests started arriving for the party, Buzz finally began to enjoy his birthday. He and his friends swung like monkeys from the apple tree in the garden.

They played a war game with lots of karate chopping and shouting.

They practised penalty shoot-outs on the lawn. So far, so good...

Then his mum came outside...in her silly spacesuit. Holding Buzz's even sillier spacesuit. "Buzz, you forgot to put this on!" she called. Buzz turned bright red.

"Wow – cool!" said Sam.

"Did you make that, Mrs Burton?" marvelled Matthew.

"Buzz, can I have a go wearing it?" begged Ben.

To Buzz's surprise, everyone wanted to try it on. Then Mr Burton got out the walkie-talkies for Buzz's friends to have a go.

"Of course, a proper astronaut would wear a space helmet as well as a spacesuit," his mum said, "but I haven't been able to make one yet." She looked thoughtfully into the kitchen. "Unless..."

Without another word, she'd sprinted inside.
Minutes later, she came out again. "Ta-da!"
she cried. "What do you think, guys?"

Buzz's eyes boggled. "What have you done
with Goldie?" he spluttered.

"Don't worry, she's in the sink," his mum said. Her voice sounded very echoey from inside the goldfish bowl. "Phew, it's hot in here." Mrs Burton pulled at the goldfish bowl. "I think I'll – oof! – get this off now...somehow..."

Buzz watched his mum's face turn red with effort as she tugged at the goldfish bowl. Then his dad had a go at getting it off.

"Ow!" yelped his mum. "Watch my chin!"

Finally, after a last enormous heave, the bowl came away. Buzz's ears went red when he heard someone sniggering, "I'm an astronaut – get me out of here!"

Great. Now everybody had realised how embarrassing his parents were. And it didn't stop there. The moon video was a disaster. George started flicking Comet Crunchies at everybody in boredom. Fred fell asleep. And Matthew tried to fast-forward to the end.

After that, Mrs Burton moonwalked
backwards into the pond during her
demonstration. It cheered everybody up at
least, but Buzz felt hot with embarrassment.

As for the 'comets and asteroids' game...
that was worst of all. The comets started
fighting the asteroids. Then the asteroids
ripped their costumes off and said they didn't
want to play any more.

"Can't we play football instead?" Buzz's
friends asked.

Later, when everybody had left, Buzz decided he had had enough, too. It wasn't just the party games and awful spacesuits. He'd had enough of being the son of astronauts. But how could he get the message across to his parents, when they were such *astronerds*?

The only way he could speak to them, he decided, was in their own language.

"Mum, Dad," he said that night over another yucky space food tea of powdered mashed potato, freeze-dried sausages and instant baked beans. "Imagine for a moment that you two are the sun..."

"What, a spinning ball of gas?" his dad guffawed. "Are you trying to tell me to stay off the beans?"

"Let him finish," Buzz's mum said. "Go on, son. Me and your dad are the sun..."

Buzz took a deep breath. "I feel like you two are the sun – and I'm Pluto!"

"You feel like you're a solid ball of rock and ice, with only a very faint atmosphere?" gulped his dad.

Buzz's mum tutted. "No, silly. He feels like he's about as far away from us as it's possible to get within the solar system," she said, biting her lip anxiously. "Is that what you mean, love?"

Buzz nodded in relief. "Yes," he said.

"Oh dear," Buzz's dad said. "That is far. In fact, it's 5,906 million—"

"I think it's brilliant that you two are going to Venus," Buzz interrupted quickly. "But it's all you ever talk about these days!

"I miss talking to you about school and football and what's on TV." He stood his fork up in his mash, and it stuck fast. "And sorry, Mum, but this space food is *awful*!"

Buzz took a deep breath and went on.
"You're going to be going away to space
soon – for weeks! Can't we keep the space
stuff out of our home until then?"

Mr Burton put his fork down. "You're
right, son. We've been getting a bit carried
away, haven't we?"

Mrs Burton put her knife down. "Sorry, Buzz. We've been so excited about Venus. But now you mention it, this tea is *terrible*. We should be making the most of proper food while we can still get it!"

She stood up. "How about I pop out to get us all fish and chips instead? Then, maybe we could all sit and watch a video together."

"Not the moon video again?" Buzz checked.

"Not the moon video," his parents chorused.

Buzz heaved a sigh of relief. "That," he said happily, feeling a tummy rumble start up at the thought of hot, crispy fish and chips, "is the best idea you've had for ages, Mum."

For their last week on Earth, Mr and Mrs Burton made a real effort to be normal. They went to the cinema, out for dinner, and did roller blading. They asked Buzz about his day at school, or talked about the things he and Grandma could do while they were away.

It was great. Buzz didn't feel embarrassed by his mum and dad all week. In fact, as the mission grew nearer, he felt proud. His parents had been chosen to orbit Venus! Even his friends seemed to have forgotten Buzz's disastrous party in the excitement.

The following Friday, it was time to say
goodbye. Buzz's grandma hugged him as they
waved his parents off. Buzz couldn't believe
they would be millions of kilometres away by
the end of the day. It felt very strange.

That afternoon, the Burtons' living room was packed. Lots of Buzz's friends had come to watch *Venturer 5* lift off, plus all the neighbours. Aunty Annie was there, with all of Buzz's cousins. It was a full house.

"There they are!" someone squeaked as the television picture panned around to show the astronauts in front of the shuttle.

Buzz squinted at the figures in white, waving from the screen. His mum and dad!

"They are sooo awesome," Danny said solemnly, and Buzz felt a shiver of pride.

"If we could just have a few words before take-off," the interviewer said. "Mr and Mrs Burton, how are you feeling?"

There was a close-up of Buzz's mum's face. She had tears in her eyes. "I just want to say...I love you, Buzzy-Wuzzy-sugar-lump. Miss you already, my little munchkin!"

Buzz coughed as everybody in the room started giggling. "Aw, *Mum*!" he groaned.

Then the camera moved along and there was Buzz's dad.

"What's he holding?" Sam asked, peering at the screen. Buzz gulped in horror. Oh, no...

"We're taking Mr Bear, our son's teddy," his dad was saying. "We're going to cuddle him at night, in place of our little Buzz."

He'd taken Mr Bear! Buzz's secret teddy that he'd never wanted his mates to find out about, ever! Even worse, somebody – his mum, it had to be – had sewn a miniature spacesuit for him!

"Mr Bear, eh?" one of Buzz's cousins hooted in amusement.

Buzz shut his eyes and held his head in his hands. The sooner his parents left the planet, the better! Just as he'd thought they'd stopped being embarrassing, they'd shown him up on national TV, to an audience of millions!

"The astronauts are now on board the shuttle," the interviewer said. "Countdown is set to begin."

"10...9...8...7...6...5...4...3...2...1...BLAST OFF!" everyone cheered.

The rocket boosters roared and the shuttle shot into the sky. Up, up, up it soared, until it was nothing but a tiny dot on screen.

"They'll be in space in eight minutes," Fred said, eyes shining. "*Wow*."

"Cool!" breathed Danny. "You're so lucky, Buzz!"

Buzz found that he was grinning. So his parents were a bit embarrassing...well, so what? He could live with it. "I *am* lucky, aren't I?" he said. "I'm the luckiest boy on Earth."

FRIGHTFUL FAMILIES

WRITTEN BY SUE MONGREDIEN • ILLUSTRATED BY TERESA MURFIN

Explorer Trauma	1 84362 563 6
Headmaster Disaster	1 84362 564 4
Millionaire Mayhem	1 84362 565 2
Clown Calamity	1 84362 566 0
Popstar Panic	1 84362 567 9
Football-mad Dad	1 84362 568 7
Chef Shocker	1 84362 569 5
Astronerds	1 84362 570 9

All priced at £8.99